Close Friends

Authoress Karma

DEDICATION

To "Jayla" Please know there are no hard feelings or bad blood. I
appreciate you for showing me how
not to be loved. For showing me what my worth was. I hope you read this
and understand why I chose to distance myself. I also want you to know
that some things you can't come back from and everything isn't meant to
be repaired. Almost is never enough. Please remember that.
Peace. Love. Karma

ACKNOWLEDGMENTS

To everyone who was inspiration in this story... Thank you

INTRO

"When you are guilty, it is not your sins you hate but yourself."
Anthony De Mello

Guilt can teach you a lot. It can eat you up or you can work with it and grow. It's funny what guilt can do to a person…It's actually hilarious. After damage is done people want to come back and fix things or make them better. When there's no point. Well expect to clear a guilty conscience. How'd the song go? It's too little too late. Certain situations you just can't come back from and that applies to both friendships and relationships. Analise learned that lesson young. She also learned to never go back to the things that break you. Analise had a hard time explaining this to a person from her past. Contacting her under the impression that they were still… associates. Analise's first heartbreak came in the form of Jayla Barnes. The five-foot four smooth talker. Analise never thought they would be in the place we are now. Not speaking nor associating. High school was forever ago, yet here she comes. Trying to make amends. What's done is done and doing things after the fact does nothing. Thinking of their last conversation on one of her many reflection days at twenty-six she was happy with life. Sure, nothing is perfect but she's in a better place. Analise was not the same naive eighteen-year-old girl Jayla used to know. She shook her head. Facebook can be a blessing and a curse these days. Jayla messaged her on Facebook last night….

Jayla: "Are you in town?"

Analise: "No."

Jayla: Damn. Well I'm coming to see you.

<u>Analise: "Nah you good."</u>

<u>Jayla: "Not an option. I'm coming.</u>

<u>Analise: "If I say you can't come to my house. Then you can't come." Period.</u>

The history between Jayla and Analise is a funny story… A story of discovery, fear and hurt. After eight years, Analise was finally able to be free of Jayla and the hurt she caused. Analise was able to build herself back up and teach her worth. Living her best life with her wife of two years in their home in Arizona overlooking the mountains. Now here she comes trying to slide her way back in. Like she had always done since the breakup all those years ago. No, not happening. Why? Well let's go back to the beginning the end of 2014… Junior year where it all began…. Where things, in Analise's life at least, began to shake up. Sitting on her balcony of her apartment; taking in the warm Arizona air. Analise thinks back to that crazy time when her world was flipped completely upside down by Ms. Jayla Barnes.

Analise was your average high school student. Not popular but she was okay with that. Popularity was overrated. The soft spoken five-foot five brown skinned beauty was content. She had her crowd and she stuck to them. School, choir, and home. That's how her days went. The day she had her first real interaction with Jayla. She was in choir practice with her best friend Bella. Everyone always called them the "weird ones" but they literally stayed in their own world. They didn't bother anyone that didn't bother them. Practice was moving at its usual pace and they had a small break. Analise took this mid practice break as the opportunity to nap. School kills the energy. So, she had her head down resting. That's when Jayla walked over.

"Excuse me?" Jayla said. Analise picked her head up, classic resting bitch face.

"Whoa… what's with the face?"
"Well I was trying to nap." Analise snapped.

"My bad." Jayla held her hands up in defense. Now, before this moment Analise and Jayla knew of each other, but they never actually talked. Jayla was more "popular" than Ana.

"I just wanted to say hi." Jayla said. "I let you rest though."

Analise had no idea but that moment would change things in a world forever. Jayla and Analise spent that day in practice talking & laughing. Harmless right? Of course, it was.

However, Analise unknowingly put herself in a line of fire she was not prepared for. Ending that day with a simple hug; it's harmless right?

Their interaction was simple and friendly. A few laughs and jokes. It all ends with a simple friendly hug. Maybe a little too friendly. At least, that's what Analise thought.

"I'm telling you Ana. She likes you." Bella said. Bella was Analise's best friend in high school. Those two were attached at the hip. One day while they were relaxing before practice. Bella was sure Jayla liked Analise.

"Now you know she don't roll like that." Ana said.

"Oh yeah? Then how come she when you get a hug from her, she wants to grab your ass. I've seen it. She doesn't hug anyone else like that. " Bella said.

"That doesn't mean she likes girls Bella."

"Sure, it doesn't." Ana shook her head. At that time, she already had a feeling, but hey you can't be too sure nowadays. Ana was open in high school. There was no shame there. She understood Bella's point. The constant close lingering hugs, the constant touching and squeezing. Maybe she was just playful. That could be it right?

1

"Do you wanna be a distraction baby?"

Kehlani

Let's just say. Hugs turned to tickling and conversations turned to flirting. It all moved so quickly. As quickly as it built up the problems came right along with it. Analise was a sweet girl and stuck with her own crowd but once she became close with Jayla people had a lot to say. Once person in particular: Dylan. For some odd reason there was the animosity there. Analise had no idea why but who cares. Dylan would make sly comments here and there. Also, she hated when Ana and Jayla were alone, talking or anything of the sort. It was all kind of bizarre how jealous she was. Jayla and Analise weren't even that close. Yet... Dylan was a problem. A big annoying problem. Analise didn't do anything to her nor did she say anything to her, yet she always picks with her. There was that day she completely crossed the line…. It was the last day of school and everyone was either leaving school or waiting to try out for a club next year. Dylan, Bella, Analise and Jayla were waiting to try out for choir again. Everyone was sitting on the stairs and Jayla had her head in Jayla's lap. Dylan was staring at the two with the look of disgust. Analise could feel the heat of her stare.

"Problem?" Ana asked.

"Ugh… Jayla come with me" Dylan demanded

"For what? Jayla questioned. She was quite comfortable.

"Please?" Dylan begged. Jayla of course agreed. The two walked around the corner of a nearby hallway. After about five minutes, Bella called Analise over to where the two were standing. Typical Bella eavesdropping… Gotta love her.

"Why she all over you anyway Jayla? I don't see why like that Bitch?" One thing you don't do is call Analise a bitch. You'll lose some teeth for sure. Yes, Analise was sweet but that temper of her's was nothing to be messed with.

"Oh, so there is a problem." Ana snapped coming over to the two.

"Chill." Jayla said. She was not in the mood for the bickering today.

"Chill? This fat muthfucka needs to watch her mouth before she gets punched in it."

"Ana, she apologizes-

"No! You apologize for her. It's cool next time she better watch her mouth." Analise walked away from the two before her anger got the best of her. Analise was a sweet girl but that temper is something else for sure. In all honesty she had no clue why she hated her so much. They barely said two words to each other all year. Analise simply chucked it up to jealousy. She's not worth getting in trouble for especially on the last day of school.

Jayla joined Analise and the others a few minutes later.

"Analise I'm sorry about her." Jayla said.

"Don't apologize. I said what I said, and I meant it. I'll punch her straight in the mouth." Analise retorted.

"Calm down killer." Bella laughed.

"Now you know neither one of us like her. She picks at us for no reason." Analise asserted.

"True, but don't stress it." Bella reminded.

"I know, but you know I hate that word. I need to use the restroom." Analise walked into the bathroom to look in the mirror. She saw Jayla standing in the door.

"Can I help you Jayla?" Jayla didn't say a word. She just stared. In an instant, Analise was pushed up against the bathroom wall. Jayla held her arms tightly.

"Seriously! You play too much Jayla."

"Do I?" Jayla laughed.

"Yes… Now let my arms go."

"No, I like this position."

Right then Ana knew… She likes girls… She likes me. Their faces almost touch… Almost. Then suddenly Jayla pulls away with a smirk.

"Don't play this game Jayla." Analise said

"Yea what if I want to play?" Jayla bit her lip and walked away. She was not about to feed into Jayla's foolishness. Suddenly, she feels Jayla grab her arm and pin her against the wall…. AGAIN! Then she smiles that perfect smile; her eyes gleaming almost in a lustful way.

"ANALISE! Samaria is out here looking for you!" Bella shouts.

"You can move now." Analise said. Jayla rolls her eyes and releases Analise's arms. She knew Analise had this little crush on Samaria. She couldn't stop that. Or could she?

As Jayla leaves the restroom, she sees Samira and Analise in a tight embrace… Jealous? Maybe. Just maybe.

"So, we're going to the beach when you're done right?" Samaria asks Analise.

"I don't know it depends on when I'm done here. I'll text

you." Samaria nodded, said her goodbyes and left.

"So, who said you could go to the beach?" Jayla questions.

"I told myself." Analise said, taking a seat on the stairs.

"Nah it don't work like that. You need my permission to go." Jayla stated. At that very moment Analise broke out in full laughter. She laughed so hard tears were falling from her eyes. She looked up at Jayla: "Oh your serious?" Analise began laughing again. Jayla knew she had no control over Analise.

They were only friends after all… For now, at least. The school year is officially over, but senior year is and will be a whole different ball game and a whole new set of problems…

2

That day in June was a memory for the two. Now into July, summer was in full swing. All nighters, sleepovers and days out shopping took up Analise's time. The two would talk almost every night. All night even. Laying across the bed ready to doze off for some sleep her phone rings: **JayBae** it read. Over the small month since school ended, Jayla and Analise grew closer. Plenty of smiles, Jokes and of course those late-night talks. "Hello? "Analise answered.

"Hey." Jayla responded.

"Hey Jay. What's up? I was about to go to sleep." Analise yawned.

"Can I get a favor?" Jayla questioned.

"Depends on what it is." Analise replied.

"Can you wake me up tomorrow for Summer School?" Jayla said.

"Really Jay?" "What did you get summer school for?"

"Attendance..."

"Yea okay... What time?"

"5:00AM"

"IN THE MORNING?" Ugh ok..."

"Thanks!"

"Welcome."

"I'll talk to you later Potential."

"Call me that again and you're on your own."

"I'm playing damn"

"Bye." Jayla has gotten into the habit of referring to Analise as "Potential". Bella was right. Jayla did like Analise. Go figure. The two spent a lot of time talking and it came out, but Jayla wasn't fully comfortable with the idea. Which Analise had a feeling that would happen. Nevertheless, the chemistry between the two was undeniable and strong. Jayla said Potential was Analise's name for the time being. Why Jayla decided to call Analise to wake her up for school no one knows, but Analise was her friend and she'll probably be up then anyway. So why not?

That following day, Analise was home relaxing under the AC when she got a text from Jayla.

JayBae: Hey Potential...

Ana: Stop calling me that!

JayBae: Can I come over?

Ana: Sure... What time?

JayBae: Around 3... Text Me the address...

Ana: Ok cool.469 S. North Ave.

Like clockwork Jayla shows up at 3pm. Analise went to open the door and there Jayla stood. "Hey."

"Wassup Ana."

"Come in... My room is the first door on the right..."

"Ooo the Goofy movie!" Jayla shouts.

"Really Jayla?" Analise looks with this quizzical look on her face at Jayla.

 She laughs. "What Goofy Movie is the shit." They sat together on my bed in a comfortable silence. Analise could feel Jayla staring a hole in her face. "Jayla why are you staring at me?" Analise asked.

"You're beautiful, "she says smiling. There's that charm again. Analise feels her cheeks get hot as she starts to blush a beet red. In a flash Jayla pulls Analise onto her lap. Analise tries to break free of Jayla's hold with no luck.

"Where are you going?" She asks. The two slowly lock eyes…. Slowly their lips connect. Suddenly Jayla pulls away.

"What's the matter?" Analise asks disappointedly.

"I shouldn't have done that. I gotta go." Jayla tries rushing off.

"Jayla what's the problem? You like me, right? "

"Of course, I do. It's just… I gotta go okay…. I'll call you tonight okay. Analise pouts. "Aye fix your face. Gimme hug." Jayla demands. Reluctantly, the two share a hug. Jayla leaves shortly after leaving Analise confused.

"The fuck just happened?" Analise asks herself.

       Later that night, Analise still hadn't heard from Jayla. Now she's worried and confused. Maybe they went too far? What if she has a girlfriend? Just then, her phone rings interrupting her thoughts, but instead of Jayla it was Samaria.

       "Yes Mari?"

"So why was Jayla at your house today?" Samaria questioned, the irritation and jealously in her voice was clear. Jayla pulled the phone away from her ear.

"The hell? You stalking me now?"

"Nah man… I was gonna stop by and see if you wanted to go get food when I saw her going into your house." Samaria explained.

"If she was here so what? I do have friends you know."

"Look just be careful… Okay?"

"Yes, okay oh great and wise Mari." Ana says sarcastically.

"Come on I'm just looking out for you. I don't want you to get hurt." Samaria said sincerely.

"We're friends Mari... That's it." Analise said.

"Yea okay…. Friends." Samaria rolled her eyes. She knew what was really going on.

"You need something else or nah?" Analise asked, clearly annoyed with Mari.

"Nah… talk to you later." With that the call ended. Analise lay in her bed watching Lifetime. Typical summer night for Analise. Suddenly, she received another call. This time it was Jayla.

"Hello?" Ana said.

"Yea wassup?"

"Late much… What if I was asleep?"

"But you're not so hush."

"So, you wanna explain what was wrong with you today and why you ran away from me like I was the Black Plague." Jayla chuckled.

"Now you're being dramatic… It wasn't like that."

"Oh yea? Explain then. Don't worry I'll wait…"

"Man look it's hard to explain." Jayla huffed.

"I wish you could see how hard I just rolled my eyes." Analise hears Jayla take a deep sigh. "Look Jayla, it's midnight and I wanna finish my movie so…. You gone explain or can I go?"

"Why you being so mean?" Jayla questioned.

"Because I can be…" Analise said.

"Look let me ask you a question." Jayla said.

"Okay…"

"Will you be my girlfriend?" The words came out of Jayla's mouth like word vomit.

"Wait what?" Analise was shocked. She was not expecting that, well at least not so soon.

"You heard me. So, what's your answer?" Jayla asserted.

"I mean yeah… I mean I uh… Analise stumbled.

"You're cute when you stutter. I'll let you go now. Text me okay?" Jayla laughed.

"Shush up about me stutter... Bye." Analise smiled.

"Bye girlfriend." Jayla said. Analise couldn't contain her excitement. Smiling so hard that her cheeks hurt. Who would have thought? Analise had a feeling but she didn't expect for things to go this far this fast. Jayla and Analise liked each other but Analise never expected Jayla to make the first move. Before heading to sleep Jayla sent Analise a simple text: ***"I won't let another minute go to waste. I want you and your beautiful soul."- Jesse McCarthy.***

3

"It can be our little secret promise you can keep it"

- Ann Marie

The summer moved quickly after that night in July. Every moment they could spend together; they were together. Analise felt like she was floating on a cloud. She was happy and in love. Jayla kept her happy. Jayla was happy. Analise was a light in her world. A date here and there. Kisses laughs and smiles filled the rest of the summer. There were no worries or stress for the two lovebirds. All is well right? Well, there was one thing that Analise couldn't forget about. They start school on Monday. How was this going to work? The thought ate away at Analise with each passing day.

Analise and Jayla hung out with two completely different crowds and before now they only hung out in choir practice. Would that change? Everyone knew Analise was into girls. She wasn't ashamed of it. It's who she was, but Jayla not so much. To top it all off, Jayla's friends didn't really like Analise that much. They thought she was weird. Which she was, but she didn't care what other people thought. She was secure in herself and whoever did not accept it didn't matter. Analise felt her concerns growing. What would happen? One day while Jayla and Analise were out taking a walk near the lakefront, Analise decided to see where Jayla's head was on the whole situation.

"Jay?" Analise questioned.
"Yes Gumdrop."

"Okay first I hate when you call me that and second you

know we start school on Monday." Analise hinted.

"Yea I know. So what?" Jayla answered.

"So, what's your plan? That's what." Analise added

"What you mean?" Jayla inquired.

"People aren't stupid Jayla. Everyone knows about me. What are you gonna do if and when it comes out that we are together?" Analise rambled.

"We'll cross that bridge when we get there. Don't worry so much." Analise rolled her eyes. Jayla was acting like it was no big deal. When it is. Whether Jayla knew it or not. It would not go over well with Jayla's little clique once it all came out. "Stop worrying so much. Jayla said. "You're doing that thing you do when you worry."

"What thing?" Analise questioned.

"You pout and wrinkle your forehead." Jayla laughed.

"I do not!" Analise folded her arms.

"Let me get you home. We do have school in two days."

"Whatever let's go." Even though Jayla tried to reassure her there was this nagging feeling Jayla couldn't shake and when she woke up for her first day of senior year it was still there. Nagging and gnawing away at her thoughts. No matter how much she tried to push them to the back of her mind it was a growing concern. The butterflies in her stomach were overflowing. Thankfully, the day seemed to go by okay. Everything went as normal. At least until lunch time, she was sitting with Bella and their classmate Jewel. Analise knew she had gotten this glow of happiness when she and Jayla started dating and boy was it noticeable.

"Ana!" Jewel shouted.

"Wassup?" Analise answered.

"Who is it?" Jewel questioned

"Stop the bull Analise. You're glowing and more smiley than usual, so who is it?" Jewel asserted.

"I don't know what you're talking about." Analise told her. The only person that knew about her and Jayla was Bella. The trio sat in a comfortable silence. Thankfully, Jewel dropped the subject or so Analise thought. Jayla and Analise had been stealing glances at each other all lunch period and she didn't know Jewel was paying attention. Jewel caught one glance and knew instantly.

"Jayla? No way!" Jewel shouted.

"Oh fuck…" Analise whispered. Shit was about to hit the fan…. Big time. The next the news of Analise spread like wildfire. Analise just kept quiet and kept her head down. Which is what she always did anyway. Analise knew trying to even remotely keep this was a bad idea. The whole day she walked through the halls, she got the glares and the whispers. She had to go to the bathroom before her next class and before she walked in, she saw two of Jayla's friends talking. "Did you hear?" One girl said.

"Hear what?" the other said.

"About Jayla and Analise?"

"Yea I don't believe it."

"Yea and when I asked Jayla, she just said that Analise liked her. That's it."

"So what? You think Analise is making it up?"

"She has to be because Jayla would never."

"If so Analise is crazy as fuck."

"For sure." The two girls exited the bathroom not even noticing Analise was right there at the door. Hurt and confused. Analise shook it off it could all just be high school gossip, right?

3

"It can be our little secret promise you can keep it"

- Ann Marie

The summer moved quickly after that night in July. Every moment they could spend together; they were together. Analise felt like she was floating on a cloud. She was happy and in love. Jayla kept her happy. Jayla was happy. Analise was a light in her world. A date here and there. Kisses laughs and smiles filled the rest of the summer. There were no worries or stress for the two lovebirds. All is well right? Well, there was one thing that Analise couldn't forget about. They start school on Monday. How was this going to work? The thought ate away at Analise with each passing day.

Analise and Jayla hung out with two completely different crowds and before now they only hung out in choir practice. Would that change? Everyone knew Analise was into girls. She wasn't ashamed of it. It's who she was, but Jayla not so much. To top it all off, Jayla's friends didn't really like Analise that much. They thought she was weird. Which she was, but she didn't care what other people thought. She was secure in herself and whoever did not accept it didn't matter. Analise felt her concerns growing. What would happen? One day while Jayla and Analise were out taking a walk near the lakefront, Analise decided to see where Jayla's head was on the whole situation.

"Jay?" Analise questioned.
"Yes Gumdrop."

"Okay first I hate when you call me that and second you

know we start school on Monday." Analise hinted.

"Yea I know. So what?" Jayla answered.

"So, what's your plan? That's what." Analise added

"What you mean?" Jayla inquired.

"People aren't stupid Jayla. Everyone knows about me. What are you gonna do if and when it comes out that we are together?" Analise rambled.

"We'll cross that bridge when we get there. Don't worry so much." Analise rolled her eyes. Jayla was acting like it was no big deal. When it is. Whether Jayla knew it or not. It would not go over well with Jayla's little clique once it all came out. "Stop worrying so much. Jayla said. "You're doing that thing you do when you worry."

"What thing?" Analise questioned.

"You pout and wrinkle your forehead." Jayla laughed.

"I do not!" Analise folded her arms.

"Let me get you home. We do have school in two days."

"Whatever let's go." Even though Jayla tried to reassure her there was this nagging feeling Jayla couldn't shake and when she woke up for her first day of senior year it was still there. Nagging and gnawing away at her thoughts. No matter how much she tried to push them to the back of her mind it was a growing concern. The butterflies in her stomach were overflowing. Thankfully, the day seemed to go by okay. Everything went as normal. At least until lunch time, she was sitting with Bella and their classmate Jewel. Analise knew she had gotten this glow of happiness when she and Jayla started dating and boy was it noticeable.

"Ana!" Jewel shouted.

"Wassup?" Analise answered.

"Who is it?" Jewel questioned

"Stop the bull Analise. You're glowing and more smiley than usual, so who is it?" Jewel asserted.

"I don't know what you're talking about." Analise told her. The only person that knew about her and Jayla was Bella. The trio sat in a comfortable silence. Thankfully, Jewel dropped the subject or so Analise thought. Jayla and Analise had been stealing glances at each other all lunch period and she didn't know Jewel was paying attention. Jewel caught one glance and knew instantly.

"Jayla? No way!" Jewel shouted.

"Oh fuck…" Analise whispered. Shit was about to hit the fan…. Big time. The next the news of Analise spread like wildfire. Analise just kept quiet and kept her head down. Which is what she always did anyway. Analise knew trying to even remotely keep this was a bad idea. The whole day she walked through the halls, she got the glares and the whispers. She had to go to the bathroom before her next class and before she walked in, she saw two of Jayla's friends talking. "Did you hear?" One girl said.

"Hear what?" the other said.

"About Jayla and Analise?"

"Yea I don't believe it."

"Yea and when I asked Jayla, she just said that Analise liked her. That's it."

"So what? You think Analise is making it up?"

"She has to be because Jayla would never."

"If so Analise is crazy as fuck."

"For sure." The two girls exited the bathroom not even noticing Analise was right there at the door. Hurt and confused. Analise shook it off it could all just be high school gossip, right?

4

"It just shatters… It keeps shattering… Nothing matters...If there's no trust between these four walls; And it's all built up on lies, it falls."

-Sevyn Streeter

Gossip is all it was to Analise; at first. Even though she continued to voice her concerns but Jayla. That smooth talker… Talked it right away. A month passed and Jayla still acted like her girlfriend. Making sure she got home safe and even spending her birthday with her. Jayla had given her a necklace that she cherished and loved dearly. Analise never took it off. Everything was right as rain, outside of school. In school, the two kept their interactions to a minimum. Something that Analise was nowhere near okay with, but hey it's high school. Since everything had come out most people who knew either thought Analise was making the whole thing up or they knew they were together. Jayla would do just enough PDA and notes here and there staying after school with Analise every so often but ask her about Analise and her response would be "Oh she just likes me. She wouldn't own up to a thing if you paid her too. Jayla was trying to keep a happy medium and it was failing.

Then, it was time for homecoming. This year, the school's choir was singing at the homecoming football game. Everything was going great aside from the fact that they would probably lose. Analise was chilling with everyone else in the choir laughing, talking and joking. The thing she did all the time when she really just wanted to be under Jayla. Of course, she and Jayla couldn't be too close, which she wasn't happy about, but she loved Jayla, so she dealt with it. No matter how much it bothered her. Then, Analise saw something that made her heart fall to her stomach. She looks over to Jayla and sees Jayla in a tight hug with her ex-girlfriend Monica. Then she saw Monica kiss Jayla on the cheek. That hurt to see. It didn't make sense. Jayla couldn't be close to her actual girlfriend, but she could be all close with her ex. Yes, they have the same friend circle but out of respect that line should not be crossed. That was a slap in the face to Analise. She felt her tears welling in her eyes. There was only one thing she could do; one person she could call....

"Hello, Samaria?" Analise whimpered.

"Analise? What's wrong?" Samaria questioned. She didn't know what was wrong, but she knew Analise was about to cry.

"Are you at the game? I need a ride home" Analise pleaded.

"Yea... Why? What happened?" Samaria asked.

"Can you just meet me at the entrance please..." Analise begged.

"Yea yea… give me ten minutes." Analise and Samaria met up a few minutes later and Samaria could see the hurt all over her face along with the dried tears. Analise rode home with Samaria in complete silence. She didn't want to talk. She was hurt. Samaria saw the tears on her face and chose to not press the issue. Samaria just decided that Analise would come around eventually. Instead she wanted to lift her up. The homecoming dance was tomorrow night after all.

"Hey, you wanna go to homecoming with me?" Samaria asked.

"Mari you know I have a girlfriend. Even though I want to ring her neck for disrespecting me and our relationship tonight, I can't do that." Analise said.

"As friends Ana. I'm not that type." Analise smiled.

"Sure." Analise agreed.

"Okay I'll pick you up at 7pm." Analise nodded. Samaria did always know how to make her feeling better.

The following night, it was time for the homecoming dance. Analise kept it simple in a plain black dress with flats and curls in her hair. Samaria arrived right on time at seven and the two left. When they arrived, Jayla, Monica and all her friends were standing outside. Jayla and Analise had been arguing since yesterday. Jayla didn't see an issue with what happened with her and Monica. To her it was no big deal. She didn't understand why Analise was upset. They are friends after all. Sure, they did date but what's the big deal? Analise chose to ignore her for the night. She didn't want Jayla's stupidity to ruin her night, it was her senior year and her last high school homecoming, no one was going to ruin it. Analise spent the entire night dancing with Mari, Bella and Jewel. Mostly, Mari and she could tell Jayla was a little bothered. Analise and Bella were taking a break when Jayla walked over.

"Analise can we talk?" Jayla asked.

"About?" Analise cut her eyes up at Jayla knowing this would be some bullshit.

"You and Mari seem close." Jayla pointed out.

"Oh? So, do you and Monica."

"That's different… I- Analise placed her hand up.

"I'm not your girlfriend... I just like you. Remember?" With that Analise walked away. Leaving Jayla stuck in her own thoughts. The rest of the night went smoothly and Analise enjoyed herself, but when she got home, she got one text... from Jayla

Jayla: I think we should break up….

The next day, Analise immediately called Jayla. Where was this even coming from?

"Hello?" She said.

"Hey Jayla… Wassup?" Analise panted.

"Nothing... I just... I'm sorry Ana." Jayla rambled.

"Sorry for what?" Jayla felt her heart fall into her stomach.

"We have way too many communication problems." Jayla added

"Wh-What?" Analise felt a lump form in her throat as she tried to hold back her tears.

"I think we should break up..." Jayla stated.

"But-- you-- this doesn't make sense. Two days ago, you said you loved me Jayla!" Analise shouted.

"I'm sorry. We can still be friends and I still would love to celebrate our anniversary. Analise sat there shocked. She's joking right

"What the fuck!" "How can you ask me that!" Analise didn't care that she was yelling. With the hot tears streaming down her face.

"Look to be honest. I-- I'm going to marry a man and have kids." There's no point in leading you on like this."

"Jayla. I love you. "You have my heart."

"I don't want it" she said sternly, and the call ended. Right then, Analise's heart shattered.

After that night, Analise lost a little of her spark. Well, all of it actually. That following Monday at school she didn't want to talk to anyone, look at anyone or be around people in general. You could see all in her face, she had been crying. It was much more than a breakup. It was what Jayla said. After everything she pulled the rug right from under her.

"Analise what's wrong?" Bella asked. Analise couldn't answer. She felt her tears prick her eyelids.

"Oh Ana… Shit Mari's coming." Bella said hoping it would convince Analise to wipe her face. It didn't.

"Analise? Why are you crying?' Mari asked as she looked at tearful Analise. All Analise could do was cry… Then right then Mari knew Jayla had broken her heart. Broken her… "Analise you gotta clean your face and I'll see you at lunch okay. It'll be okay. She's not worth it." Analise knew Samaria was right but she was too hurt to think logically at the moment. Then, as she was heading to class, she ran into Jayla...Great… She quickly ran the opposite direction. If Jayla knew what was best for her… She'd stay far away from Analise.

Throughout the day Jayla saw Analise; not one word

spoken between the two. She didn't hurt her that bad… Did she? Unbeknownst to Jayla, Analise was broken… Shattered. That once happy glowing face was stained with tears. Sure, they were having problems but to go from "I love you." to a breakup was something Analise never expected. Jayla went about her day as usual. Yes, she felt bad, but it was she felt she needed to do. It was for the best right? The word had begun to spread about the "break up", even though there were some who still thought Analise was flat out lying; those who knew the real story we're pissed at Jayla. Analise was a nice girl. She didn't deserve Jayla pulling the rug right from under because she could own up to her shit. Jayla felt that this was the best decision for her at least… It had to be. Though it was best for Jayla Analise, on the other hand was breaking down; mentally, physically and emotionally. Every little thing Jayla did set Analise off and Jayla would try to make things better. Be there and provide comfort but it would make Analise angrier…. Bitter… Analise was just broken.

5

" No one ever made me feel this way. I lost myself in you from the very first day. Now I'm left feeling so confused." -Olivia

Time moved swiftly for the two. Almost like a blur; with senior year being a stressful time with college just around the corner there was really no time for distractions. Unfortunately, distractions always filled Analise's day. Mentally she had checked out. Analise did her best to avoid Jayla which failed, since Jayla insisted on being around Analise, but they also had three classes together and choir after school. So, that proved rather difficult. Analise would play little games with Jayla just to see if she was over Analise and even though Jayla would get jealous petty even, but it was too little too late for that. Slowly, Analise began the healing process, but one day Analise saw something that took her by shock… All of the breath left her body… THE walls started to cave in, and her chest hurt. The breath left her body. That day in the halls of the school Analise saw Jayla and Monica locked in a deep embrace. Right then, the hard work she put into healing went out the window. The air in her lungs left and she turned pale. The tears threatened to spill. Analise quickly ran away. She didn't know where she was going, but she knew she had to get away. She first ran into the bathroom hoping to calm down enough, but that failed when she heard: "Analise!" Jayla shouted. Great. Why couldn't she just leave well enough alone.

"What Jayla?" Analise gritted.

"Can we talk?"

"Oh, now you wanna talk? Fuck you and that talk!" Analise shouted as she punched the bathroom stall. The door went flying, almost hitting Jayla in the face. Yes, her hand was in pain, but she didn't care. She just wanted Jayla to leave her alone. "Get away from me Jayla. I mean it. Stay away from me." Analise walked out that day hoping that Jayla got the message. Jayla stood in the bathroom stunned. She didn't think it was that bad. The look of pure anger and hurt was all over Analise's face. How did it get this bad? The darkness Jayla saw in Analise's eyes told her everything she needed to know.

"Jayla you might wanna get out here." Bella said. Jayla walked out into the hallway to see Analise with her backpack in her hand. The school was empty, clubs had ended and almost everyone had gone home besides everyone in choir. Suddenly, Analise took Jayla's backpack and dumped its contents up and down the hall.

"You get it now?!" Analise shouted. LEAVE ME ALONE!" With that she grabbed her things from the classroom and left. Analise didn't care what trouble she got into. She just hoped Jayla got the message. Jayla stood in the hall watching Analise leave with the feeling of shock and disappointment overtaking her as she began to collect her things.

6

"Don't tell me you're sorry 'cause you're not. Baby when I know you're only sorry you got caught."
Rihanna

The next day, Analise was doing her hair, getting ready for the event they had today; when she got a text message: **IGNORE□□□: Sit next to me on the bus we need to talk.** Analise's first thought is What the fuck we gotta talk about? Knowing it's Jayla. She ignores the message and continues getting ready for the event. Analise got to the school so they could catch the bus to the competition. She sees Jayla and ignores her while she was looking for Bella. "Where the hell is Bella?" She thought to herself. Bella was her bumper so she could avoid Jayla at all cost.

"Time to load the bus!" Mr. C, our teacher, yells. Analise gets on the bus and sits in the back and of course here comes Jayla plopping downright next to her. Bella was nowhere in sight.

"Thank god for headphones!" Analise thought to herself. Once the bus pulls off Jayla takes one of her headphones out of her ear. Analise stays stoic as quiet as a mouse.

"Ana?" Jayla says.

....

"Analise!" Jayla shouts. Analise just shoots her a glare.

"Can we talk?" Jayla asks. Analise places her headphones back in her ears. Once again Jayla takes them out and then she takes Analise's phone in the. So, Analise just looks out the window.

"Analise... I'm sorry about last night." Analise's thoughts were: "Yea whatever." She remained silent and rolled her eyes.

"You know we argued about that." Jayla tells her.

"Okay Jayla & what?" Analise says.

"I'm sorry..." Jayla mumbles

"I'm sick of hearing that. That's all you can ever say to me." Analise felt a tear roll out of her eye. She quickly wiped it away. She started to talk but by then the bus had stopped. "Jayla you can say you're sorry all you want, but nothing is going to change between us afterwards. Is it?

Jayla just sat there silently. Knowing what Analise and what she wanted. As much as Jayla wanted her back. She couldn't bring herself to admit it.

"That's what I thought." Analise said as she walked to the front of the bus. Analise was sick of all of Jayla's fake apologies. Apologies mean nothing without changed behavior. The event came and went. Jayla wasn't sure what to do next. She did know that Analise was right. Sure, she apologized but what was next? What would change? Jayla didn't know. So, that day she decided to take Analise's advice and leave her alone. Maybe distance is what's best for both of them. No matter how much Jayla wanted things to be okay. They wouldn't be.

7

"Why her? Why her? Did I get on your nerves? Did I give you too much that you couldn't handle my love?"

-Monica

Months passed… Prom came and went pretty soon the end of the year was rearing its head. Jayla kept her distance, well as best she could. For some reason she couldn't seem to leave Analise alone and, even though it annoyed her, Analise didn't mind it. It only further proved the point that Jayla did like her regardless of the things she said. Analise's plan was to not let Jayla ruin the last of her senior year. The senior class was about to head out on their senior trip. Bella, Analise and Jewel were ready to let loose and celebrate their graduation. Nothing could go wrong… Right?

Well…. That didn't go as planned. Why? Let's start with the first night. The teachers decided that Sky zone would be a good fit. Everyone could run around and jump to their heart's content. Literally. Everything was going great. Bella and Analise were attached at the hip of course and She and Mari had gotten really close since homecoming. Analise was nowhere near ready for something serious. She wasn't over Jayla just yet… Well, at all really. The whole situation really stung. Mari understood that, however. Mari knew Analise was worth waiting for, so she did just that. Mari felt that there was no rush, they had time… All the time in the world.

Analise and Bella were in their own world as always, playing in the ball pit.

Ana!" Think Fast!" Bella yells. The soft ball bounced right off Analise's head.

"Hey no fair! "Analise laughs. Then she takes a look in the wrong direction. She saw Jayla and Monica. Monica was laying on top of Josiah while she was on the trampoline. Okay that hurt.... So much for no PDA.

"Hey look at me." Let's keep jumping." Bella says. Analise's mood soured just a bit but she tried to shake it off. "What was so great about Monica?" The feeling of doubt washed over her. "Why her? Why not me?" She thought. Then like clockwork…Here comes Jayla.

"Hey." Jayla says.

"Wassup." Analise replied.

"What's wrong with you?" Jayla questioned.

"Nothing." where's Monica?" Analise snapped.

"Here we go!" Jayla shouted, catching Mari`s attention. Seeing Analise and Jayla; she thought it'd be best if she got over there and fast.

"Goodbye Jayla! Just leave me alone." Analise could feel the tears pricking her eyes. Not again. She thought she was past crying.

"Analise you know why we broke up… I'm sorry. it's--." She says.

"It's what Jayla? Please spare me with you bullshit today. Go play kissy face with your girlfriend!" Analise shouted. Analise walked away once again and she was worked up. She bumped straight into Mari.

"Ana what's wrong? Mari asks. Analise couldn't get any words out. The tears just started coming.

"Jayla again?" Mari says. Mari pulls Analise into a hug knowing that's what she needs. Analise didn't need to say a word it was all over her face.

"Analise!" Jayla shouted. Seeing Mari and Analise close just rubbed Jayla the wrong way but she shook it off. She had to make sure Analise was okay, she didn't want her upset with her...Well not more than she already was.

"Look Jayla you've done enough damage just give her

some space okay?" Mari told Jayla. Glaring at Mari Jayla agreed only because she knew she could talk to Analise when she was crying… They would talk… Eventually. Analise knew its best for her to keep some distance and collect her thoughts.

"Analise… When you do talk to her. Let her know everything. Every emotion. Let it out because Bella and I miss you… The you before the hurt and, you know, even if Jayla doesn't want you. I do." Mari told her as she gently kissed her forehead. Analise with a tear stained face felt her heart flutter ever so slightly. Analise took that night to have some serious reflection time. She thought about what she wanted to say and what she needed to get off her chest. Sitting on the windowsill of her room Analise got her thoughts together. Tomorrow was the last day. It was all or nothing. Even though everything went completely wrong she was happy with Jayla. Some of her happiest moments were with Jayla. She had one last chance and tomorrow she would take advantage. All she could do was try…. What could it hurt?

The next night, it was yearbook signing time. All the seniors were saying goodbye and excitement was everywhere. So, in all the craziness Analise thought this would be the perfect moment to talk to Jayla. No one would be paying attention. Of course, Jayla agreed. The two slipped away into Analise's room. Analise on one side. Jayla the other. The two stared at each other briefly. The tension in the air was thick mostly because of Analise's nerves.

"Jayla I---" Analise takes a deep breath to calm her nerves.

"I know what you said... But I can't let it go that easily. I love you and... I... Want my... I want. My baby back... I'm not acting like this just... To be dramatic... It. Hurts… How could you just drop me like I'm nothing? Like we were nothing. It makes no sense to me. So, you gotta throw me a bone or something." Analise let the tears fall as she talked. Even Though she said she wouldn't cry. She did, but she didn't care. Suddenly, there was a knock on the door. Analise quickly wiped her face and went to see who it could be.

"Hey Ana. "Monica said.

"Hey Mo." Analise replied with a lone tear still sitting in her eye.

 "You okay?" Monica asked.

"Yea. I'm fine." Analise told her.

"Well if you wanna talk I'm here. I know we are not that cool but if you need a shoulder I'm here."

"Thanks." Ana said. Analise closed the door and looked at Josiah. She knew people were looking for her. Now, it was all in Jayla's court.

Jayla Analise was hurt, but she hadn't fully grasped the situation. In her mind she did what she could before the relationship, during and after. She could see the hurt and it was never her intentions to break Analise down like this, but they just can't be. \`\`Analise... I'm sorry... I understand where you're coming from. But we.... Can't be...I love you I do. But I can't...." Jayla said. Hearing those same words once again, proved that no matter what… nothing would change. There was nothing she could do.

"Ana come here." Jayla called to her. Analise walked over to Jayla and just cried into her shirt. Jayla held her close. At that moment, Jayla felt all the pain through her tears. She kissed her forehead once she calmed down and Jayla left...This was it… it was really over…. In that moment, Jayla realized there was nothing she could do. She wanted things to be okay; to be better, but sorry was only a temporary bandage. It didn't fix anything. It just covered up the scar.

8

And I just wanna hold you all night long… Whenever I'm around you, nothing's wrong….

-Queen Naija

Deep down, Jayla felt bad. She didn't want it to end this way, but unfortunately it has to be this way. As she's making her way back down to the common area with the rest of her classmates, she runs into Samaria.

"Aye Jayla?" Samaria asked. Jayla just looked up almost like she was in a daze. "Where's Analise Jayla?" Samaria questioned.

"She's in her room." Jayla stated as she walked away to join the other, her thoughts a jumbled mess. Samaria made her way upstairs to Analise's room. At first, she gently knocked before realizing that the door was open. There she saw Analise with her headphones in and her face buried in a pillow. Samaria made her way over and just gently rubbed Analise's back, causing Analise to glance up. For a moment, the two stared at each other. Analise took in all of Mari for the first time in a while. From her rich caramel skin to her smoldering dark brown eyes and long black hair. Standing at five foot six, Samaria was very easy on the eyes. The stare was intense. Samaria looked into Analise's tearful eyes before speaking. "It went bad didn't it?" Analise just nodded letting the tears fall." It's okay Analise…you're gonna be okay. I'm here and so is Bella." Mari just hugged Analise as a way to let her know she was there and unlike Jayla, she wasn't going anywhere.

Samaria had butterflies erupting in her stomach. Samaria had a thing for Analise for years. She just didn't know how to act on it. It took three years for the two of them to become as close as they did, but good things take time. Samaria knew what she wanted and Analise was it. She didn't care how long it took, how long she had to wait; in the end Analise would be hers. Samaria wasn't going to rush anything, especially since Jayla had basically broken Analise in almost every way. She had to be patient and help Analise build herself back to up. She wanted Analise to be the best she could be.

Samaria saw the great potential in Analise even though she didn't see it within herself. Samaria was going to make sure no one could ever break that beautiful spirit or dim that gorgeous light in eyes again. Samaria was the type to see something that she wanted and go after it. The right way. Samaria was going to take her time and at some point, it will all fall into place. Letting Analise heal was the first step in Samaria's plan, because she knew once Analise got over this; she would be unstoppable. It was just going to take time.

"Samaria?" Analise whispered.

"Yes Ana?"

"Thank you… I know I've been pretty much a triggered mess lately but thank you for being there for me." Analise smiled.

"You know it's no problem and if I'm completely honest…. I knew I should have said something way before now but... I like you Analise… A Lot. Samaria rambled. "I know you're nowhere near ready to be hear any of this but. Just know… when you're ready… I'll be here." Samaria continued. Analise stood in Samaria's arms in somewhat of a shock. Yes, she did have a crush on Samaria but, she felt like Samaria was way out cf her league. Samaria Matthews, the five-foot six softball player with a smile that could melt all hearts; wanted Analise. Looking into those beautiful brown eyes once again, Analise felt her body heat up. She knew she was blushing red and small smile creeped up on her face.

"Ah see there it is... That smile that I love so much." Samaria's face happily lit up seeing Analise smile for the first time in a while... Well genuinely anyway.

"You okay enough to go have some fun?" Samaria asked. Analise nodded. "I need to go clean my face first." Analise said. Samaria released her hold on Analise to let her get herself together. The two walked out of Analise's room together ready to live up the night and they did just that.

How'd the rest of the night go? Yearbooks were signed and tears were shed. Happy tears for some and tears of sadness for others. High school was officially over and done with. Analise knew she needed to let everything with Jayla go and move on. There was no turning back. It was far from easy. On the way back home, Analise cried and when she got home, she cried again. She would make this her last and final cry over Jayla. It was time to let it all go and move on. College would be starting soon after all. This was a time for Analise to reinvent herself and grow stronger. She was sad and broken yes, but knowing that there was a possibility with Samaria, may have helped push her into a better direction. It was time to start building herself back up and letting all the hurt go.

For Jayla, she knew she was wrong. She knew she loved Analise. She knew she wanted Analise, but something was holding her back. Jayla wanted more than anything to right her wrongs, but at this point it was too late. Especially after what she said to Analise on their last night together. It broke her heart to see Analise so hurt, but this was for the best. The two would be on separate paths. Different colleges and different friends. Jayla wanted to focus on herself and get herself together. "Maybe it's best I forget Analise?" She thought. Jayla knew it wouldn't be possible to forget that bubbly spirit and that bright smile, but for now it was time to forget all that and focus on what's ahead. Maybe one day… they would find their way back to each other. How'd the saying go? "If the love real it'll find its way back."

Analise stood on her balcony looking at her Facebook

messenger, looking at the conversation between her and Jayla. The trip down memory lane had pulled her away from the conversation for a moment.

Analise: I'm in a relationship Jayla.

Jayla: I am too, and I want you to meet her. You played such a big role in my life, especially high school.

Analise looked at her phone thinking What the actual fuck? They broke up seven years ago. Why should she… No, why would she meet her current girlfriend. That makes no sense. It had been almost a year since they had even contacted each other. What was the point?

- **_Analise: Look Relationship or not I've washed my hands of you. You did what you did too little too late we won't ever be cool or close again One thing I've learned to never go back to things that broke you Just act like I don't exist._**

- **_Jayla: That is fair, and I respect that. I hope one day you will forgive me and realize that I never meant to hurt you or break you. Me denying our relationship that day was the dumbest thing I've ever done. I was too afraid to be openly gay and I let that fear hurt someone that meant so much to me. With everything in me, I am so sorry. Being_** *with you that summer was the best memories I have in high school. You are truly an amazing young lady and thank you for opening your world to me.*

- *Analise: I already forgave you for my own sake and sanity. I just can't have your energy around me anymore.*
- *Jayla: I hate that my fear is what hurt you. I hate that I was too afraid to be out. I realized that what bothered me the most about that day was that I felt outted. Yeah people could tell that I liked girls, but I never really got the chance to come out myself. At the end of the day, it is your world and you don't have to invite me in.*

- *Analise: I never outed you I never ever said You were my girlfriend people figured it out on their own. I knew it was a bad idea for me to date someone closeted because I'm not okay with being a secret Ever What hurt me was you saw me breaking and because you were so scared you made me the fall guy. You didn't care as much as you say if you did that, I can't put myself through that anymore. And that's facts. I know better now.*

-

- *Jayla: I never said you outed me. The whole thing spread like wildfire. I was getting questioned left and right. I didn't know what to do or what to say. I tried to explain that to you and all you seemed to care about was not being claimed. There was no way I could keep us a secret. Our chemistry was too strong, and I was always checking for you. When you were breaking, I was right there! I kept bothering you. I kept coming to (lol that signing shit after school that I cannot think of the name to save my life) I would be at school at 5:30am for Softball. Stay at school all fucking day. Then go to the choir thing. bus to make sure you were good. I would get off a block up from your stop to get on the other bus to go east. I was there and you never knew. I cared so much for you.*

-

- *Analise: Not after we broke up You weren't Not being claimed wasn't the issue My issue was that you one let me be the fall guy for your fear and not only that I felt like when I found out that people thought that I was crazy Then you were ashamed of me and if you didn't notice when we broke up I didn't want you anywhere near me Then you turn around and date Monica. Biggest slap in my face So please spare me with what you thought you did to be there. Senior year was stressful enough but then I had people saying I was crazy and all that on top of the other bs I had to put up with. Lesson learned for sure and even Years after we broke up, I had people contacting me anonymously calling me crazy so again spare Me*

Yes, even after the breakup people were still harassing her online a year later. All anonymously of course. High school was over, yet people were still on Analise. Analise was the bad guy. The one in the wrong. The only thing she did wrong was love the wrong person, Jayla just couldn't understand it. This wasn't the first time Jayla tried to come back in Analise's life. Hell, it wasn't even the third or fourth. Analise stood there shaking her head as her mind did wander off to the first failed attempt.

9

" It's funny how the tables turn now it's you running after me."

-Monica

Yes, Around December in 2015 Jayla made her first of many attempts. Little did Jayla know. The Analise she thought she knew was long gone. Analise was home from her first semester of school when she got a message from Jayla asking her to come over. Over the school year they were cordial. They talked here and there. Analise would consider them associates. Jayla They could hang out. What's the harm in that? Analise was also in a relationship. With you. Well, Samaria of course. They had only been together a month or so. Still taking things very slowly because Samaria went out of state for college. Samaria kept her word; she was there for Analise that entire her summer. She even had her back through all the anonymous social media attacks. Analise had to honor her for that. Even Though she hadn't fully healed, Analise decided to give Samaria a chance. So far, everything was perfect and Analise was genuinely happy.

Back to Jayla, she was also home for the Christmas holiday, and she wanted to see Analise. Analise agreed. They were cordial after all. When Jayla arrived, Analise was watching tv. Chicago had a fresh white blanket of snow on the ground. Jayla spoke to Analise's mom before heading back to her room. The two sat together on Analise's bed in a comfortable silence. Jayla did what she always did. Stare. Of course, Analise could feel the eyes on her, but she was not about to entertain Jayla's foolishness. Jayla slowly moves closer to Analise and leans in like she wants a kiss… Analise pulls her head away.

"Nope." Analise tells her. Jayla stops only for a few minutes. Then she moves in again only to be denied once more.

"Come on man." Jayla huffed.

"No Jayla." Analise responded, rolling her eyes.

"Why?" Jayla questioned. Utterly shocked that Analise turned her down. "What changed?" She wondered.

"We're friends, right?" Analise asked. Jayla nodded. "Friends don't kiss each other." Analise stated. Jayla huffed and sat back on the bed. Irritation was written all over her face. What did she think would happen? Very shortly after, Jayla was leaving; blaming the weather as an excuse to leave. When in reality she was a little upset that Analise shot her down. "What changed?" Jayla asked herself once again.

Right as Jayla left, Analise texted Samaria; she had already informed her that Jayla was coming over.

Analise: Jayla just left.

Mari: Yea. what happened?

Analise: Well, she tried to kiss me… twice. No worries though. I shut that down.

Mari: I know you did. I trust you… Analise smiled at the message. She was grateful that Samaria trusted her around Jayla. It warmed her heart. That was the good thing about their relationship, with Samaria being in California for school, trust was very important, and it was something they definitely had with each other.

Now Jayla was shocked and disappointed but did think that was going to stop her. Not in the slightest. She loved Analise and she didn't want to give up just yet. She couldn't.

A few weeks passed since that day. Analise made the conscious decision to keep all interactions with Jayla limited out of respect for her relationship. It was a cold winter's night and Analise was home watching How the Grinch Stole Christmas when she got a call from Jayla. They hadn't really spoken since she tried to kiss her two weeks ago.

"Hello?" Analise answered.

"Can we talk?" Jayla asked.

"Okay talk?" Analise responded

"No in person. Where are you right now?" Jayla stated.

"Home." Analise said plainly.

"Home home or grandma house home?" Jayla questioned knowing Analise was playing games.

"I'm at home. What do you want?" Analise questioned already knowing Jayla was up to something.

"I told you… I want to talk." Jayla said again.

"Okay so talk. We don't need to meet face to face." The line was silent. "Jayla I'm gonna gonna go now. Bye" Analise hung up quickly. Jayla sat in her car; contemplating on what to do next. She knew there was no way to get Analise out of the house. So instead of doing what she wanted to. She took a deep breath and made another phone call.

"Analise?" Jayla sighed.

"What Jayla?" Analise answered. She was annoyed at this point.

"I realized some things lately. I know where my head is and what's important. I know what I want and what I want to do, What I need to do." Jayla took a deep breath. "I got you something. Can you come downstairs?"

"Okay… "Analise responded

"I got you a promise ring…." Jayla blurted out. Analise sat silently. Jayla sat there and waited for Analise to give her an answer. She hoped it would be the one she wanted to hear.

10

"So, I hear you wanna fix us? Should've act right back when I gave a fuck."

" - Ann Marie

"I got you something. Can you come downstairs?"

"Okay… Wait a minute… Are you at my house right now? What the hell Jayla. "Analise responded

"I got you a promise ring…." Jayla blurted out. Analise sat silently. Jayla sat there and waited for Analise to give her an answer. She hoped it would be the one she wanted to hear. Analise sat on the phone for a moment and her exact thoughts were: "Your joking, right?' She wanted to burst out in laughter.

"Jayla… no." Analise snipped trying to hold in her laughter.

"I mean I know we had it rough, but I want another chance." Jayla begged.

"It's too late for all this. Whatever this is that you're trying to do." Analise said.

"Better late than, never right?" Jayla responded.

"Wrong. Goodbye Jayla." Analise hung up and let laughter consume her. Jayla had to be joking. Now after almost a year she's ready. Yea right. Analise could help but laugh, but in a way, she had a feeling this would happen. All that time in high school Jayla wouldn't own up to anything and now all of a sudden Analise is supposed to forgive and forget. Analise wasn't ready to do that. She wasn't there yet. Analise didn't know when she would fully forgive Jayla or if she ever would. She had Samaria now. She didn't need Jayla.

She quickly called Samaria.

"Mari?!" She shouted.

"Wassup Ana banana?" Samaria answered.

"You will never guess what happened!" Analise began.

"What happened?" You okay? Samaria asked, almost nervous.

"I'm fine… Are you ready to laugh?" Analise told her ready to laugh

"Come on... What is it?" Samaria asked anxiously. Analise explained what just happened with Jayla all while laughing.

"You're joking right?" Samaria questioned.

"I wish I was my love." Analise wiped a tear that had fallen from her eye during her laughing fit.

"Well she had her chance and blew that… You're with me now. I'm not even gonna trip over Jayla and her flip flopping. Analise nodded agreeing and then changed the conversation. Jayla was a non-factor at this point.

Outside, Jayla didn't know what to do. She didn't expect Analise to say no. What would she do now? She sat in her car. Lost in her thoughts. What should she do next? She didn't know. Maybe it was too late. Or maybe she'd give Analise some time. Whether Analise knew it or not Jayla did love her. She'd wait, because if it's real it would come back. Right?

After that night, Analise and Jayla barely spoke. Well, they didn't speak at all. They both were in school. They had their own lives and their own focuses. Heads down and the work did begin. Analise not only had school but she had Samaria and when the spring semester rolled around something changed. Analise started to notice a change in Samaria. One she didn't like. They were arguing more, and Samaria had suddenly turned secretive. Had Analise done something? She didn't know. Was she being too clingy? All these doubts swam through her mind. Then one day it came crashing down. Analise discovered Samaria had cheated on her; via social media and sad to say this was not the first time. Analise was tired of forgiving. "Maybe it was her fault?" She'd thought. Maybe she was unlovable. Something had to be wrong with her. Maybe this was her Karma for choosing Samaria over Jayla. Who knows? After the breakup with Samaria took a step back from relationships to work on herself. Get better and find herself again. After two stabs to the heart. She needed to heal. Big time.

11

" You think you love me now... I think you should be worried."

-Kehlani

A year quickly passed, Analise and Jayla kept their communication sparse. Still dealing with her breakup with Samaria. Analise was on this downward. She still kept her grades up as best she could, but she was drinking… a lot. When she would get drunk for some reason, she would call Jayla. Sad but true. They would talk and laugh and joke like old times, but unbeknownst to Jayla Analise wasn't herself. She was far from herself. Analise was falling apart and she needed to pull it together and fast. It was so hard. Analise just wanted to forget all her problems. All her pain. Analise kept it hidden well, but when Thursday nights came around it was on. Jayla of course enjoyed speaking to Analise when she behaved this way, but when she would try to talk to Analise sober it would always end in an argument about the past and all Jayla wanted to do was move forward. However, Analise wasn't ready for that yet.

About two months into the second year of school, Samaria did end up reaching out to Analise. Apologizing yet again for cheating… Again. The back and forth was getting old and Analise was over it all. Samaria needed to make up her mind and figure out if she wanted to be single or not. Analise not being in the clearest headspace let Samaria have another chance, but this time if she cheated. Analise would have a plan of her own for Samaria. She wouldn't be dumb anymore and Samaria would learn that lesson the hard way, whether Samaria knew it or not. Surprise surprise… Samaria cheated again. This was the third time. Analise found out via Instagram, but she didn't call Samaria out this time. She kept it to herself and finished the school year letting Samaria think everything was right as rain.

The second year of college flew for everyone. Especially Analise, she spent most of the time in a daze; only focused when she needed to be. Now, she was home for the summer. As always, she was home; engrossed in the tv. Yes, she was still in a relationship with Samaria, but just like Samaria she decided she wouldn't be the only one with side pieces. The biggest difference is Analise knew how not to get caught. Analise was watching Catfish when she got a text from Jayla.

Jayla: Can I come over? Analise smiled, but on the inside she did feel guilty. She told herself she would never be a cheater, but she figured Samaria deserved it. Plus, Jayla was so willing to "try again" so Analise thought...Why not? So yes, she was in a relationship with Jayla and Samaria. Very unlike her, but she didn't care.

Analise: Yea sure, Analise responded.

Jayla: Can I stay the night? Analise quickly texted yes knowing her mom wouldn't mind. Then, since she was having company, she decided to quickly make tacos for dinner. About an hour later Jayla showed up. The two got comfortable in her room before Jayla asked: "Hey, can you fix me some tacos?" Analise looked perplexed.

"No, I cannot. Both your legs work, and you not company no more. I'll go to the kitchen with you that's it. Analise said, looking at Jayla like she had two heads.

"You serious?" Jayla questioned.

"As a heart attack." Jayla chuckled and the two went downstairs and had dinner together.

"You know I love you right?' Jayla said as the two of them laid in bed cuddling. Analise just smiled but looked down feeling a tiny amount of guilt. She knew she was with Jayla for the wrong reasons.

"What's wrong?" Jayla asked, noticing Analise's mood change.

"Oh, it's nothing. I'm okay." Analise told her. Then she placed a small kiss on her lips. The night went well. Did Analise cheat? Yes, she did, and she felt like shit after. The whole night with Jayla she thought about Samaria. She knew she was wrong, but she was tired of Samaria cheating on her. Analise will come clean unlike Samaria. She wanted a reaction out of her, and she didn't care what the consequences were. Analise just wanted to prove a point. Analise did exactly what she said she would do.

 She told Samaria a week later… How did that go exactly…? Well, Samaria came home for a visit about a week later and Analise met her down by the beach…. The waves were calm, the breeze was nice, but there was a small amount of tension in the air.

"I missed you." Samaria said. Analise smiled warmly, but she had guilt eating her up. Yes, she made a choice to teach Samaria a lesson but doesn't mean she doesn't feel remorse she is human. "I missed you. So, you make any new friends this time around?" Analise jumped right into it. Knowing Samaria was about to lie.

"Nah you know me I had sports and my number one girl to worry about." Samaria said. That sly devil. Analise knew she was full of it. "Oh, so you don't know… Um what's her name? Keyona. Samaria froze. She wasn't expecting that at all. "What are you talking about bae?" Samaria questioned.

"Oh, don't bae me. You know exactly what I'm talking about! Keyona! You know your girlfriend! The one you've been running around Cali with!"

"Ana baby. I-

"Save it Samaria Grace! You really need to learn to do better with your cheating." Samaria stood in front of Analise stuck. "It's okay. I cheated too." Analise laughed.

"You what?!" Samaria shouted. Analise stood with a smirk.

"You heard me. I. cheated. On. you. Did you get it that time?" Analise laughed. Samaria ran her hands through her hair. The anger written on her face. It was like she had steam coming from her ears. "Who was it?" Samaria questioned.

"Don't worry about it." Analise laughed. Samaria's face was red, and she was pissed.

"Who was it? Either tell me or I know your lying." Samaria stated hoping to call Analise's bluff.

"You wanna know? Fine. It was Jayla." Analise stated confidently.

"What? You cheated on me with the girl that was ashamed of you. The girl who broke you! The girl that had everyone thinking you were crazy! Really?" Samaria shouted. Analise stood there stone faced. What Samaria said was true and it hurt but in that moment; Analise wouldn't let it show.

"Yea I did it and I enjoyed it. Analise didn't enjoy it. Hell, Jayla even asked her why she didn't orgasm, and she didn't have an answer for her. It was good temporary relief but Analise genuinely felt bad.

"Oh, so since you enjoyed it go be with her, I'm done with this. I'm done with you." Samaria stormed off to her car fuming. As soon as Samaria walked away Analise broke down. All the times Samaria cheated and the one-time Analise gives her a taste of her own medicine it's a problem. Sure, it was worse because it was Jayla, but it was one time. Both of them were wrong and two wrongs don't make a right.

Samaria was pissed. She drove around the city in a rage. She never expected Analise to cheat. Okay, that's a lie she did, but she didn't expect it to be Jayla. She also never expected to cheat either. Especially after working so hard to pursue Analise. Samaria was unsure of what happened. When she got to college, she completely lost focus. This felt like a stab to the heart. Just because it was Jayla. Samaria needed time to think and so did Analise.

12

"You left the best you had. Now you're gonna act like that."

- LeToya Luckett

Analise sat on her balcony laughing at the memories of her and Jayla. Jayla didn't even know that she was basically a side chick. After that day, it was back to limited contact. Sometimes Analise did slip up and call Jayla, but as of lately it had been a year since they last talked and here Jayla comes from this mess… Again. Jayla had finally responded to Analise's last message bringing her attention back to the conversation at hand.

Jayla: I WAS NEVER ASHAMED. I hate that you even thought that. Idk what a fall guy is? Nobody thought you were crazy. They thought at first that you were lying because I was more popular than you. I heard it from their mouths. Who was telling you this? They lied to you. Monica and I were not together. We were just fucking around. We never asked each other out. I did all that shit well after we broke up. Somebody contacted you and said what?

Analise: Coulda fooled the hell outta me. And I got a message back in college freshman year and it said something like why you are so obsessed with Jocelyn it's clear she doesn't even like you. Your crazy. I had all the bs thrown at me because of you and you want us to be cool □right. Oh, I got other one that said: It's crazy to love someone who doesn't even like you. Fall guy is when someone takes bs and blame for another person's fuck ups. So, like I said spare me I know My worth now back then I didn't

Jayla: Man, only if you truly knew. I wish I could take you back in time and show you what was really going on. Show everything

I did to make sure that you weren't the "fall guy" You never needed help coming back at people.

Analise: Whatever you did Didn't help because people already had their minds made up about me

Jayla: Clearly, I didn't do enough and for that I'm sorry. It truly seems like you can only see this from 1 way. I understand that. Again, it is your world and I'm grateful for the moments you shared it with me. I will always regret hurting you 7 years ago. I hope one day we can just meet up and hash it all out and repair what is broken between us. Until then I wish you nothing but greatness for you in all you do.

Analise cocked her head to the side. Is she serious? All she had to do was OWN her truth. Say yes, we are together. This my girlfriend and stand up of Analise whether Analise could handle herself or not. It's a respect thing. A respect for Analise and their relationship as a whole. It's the principle and Jayla just didn't seem to get it.

Analise: One way? How else am I supposed to see it when I got so Much shit from it My first genuine heartbreak taught me a lot and there is nothing to repair because the girl you knew no longer exist

Jayla: I'm not looking for the same girl. I want to get to know the person you have become. I am not the same person from high school either. The decisions I made in high school has already been done. For those that I wronged during that time, I can only apologize and hope that my apologies are accepted.

Analise: Like I said I forgave you I won't ever forget It was so much pain there that I won't forget It was all too little to late go

<u>on and let me go because I'm not changing my mind. I'm done.</u>

With that, Analise did what she should've done years ago, she blocked Jayla. There was no need for any continued contact. Analise had been through a lot over those seven years. She made the decision to forgive Jayla about two years ago. Why? It was time. Analise had been to therapy and there she figured out just how deeply Jayla had hurt her. Analise had become unsure within herself and even more insecure. She didn't trust anyone anymore. She was in relationship and the damage Jayla did scarred deeply. It almost ruined her marriage. Analise's therapist gave her the tools to get herself back together. So, in order to fix herself completely she forgave Jayla. One day, Analise sat down wrote a letter it read:

Dear Jayla,

It's been what 5-6 years now? You still have this hold on me. Why? I don't know. I hated you for a long time. All you had to do was love me unconditionally and unapologetically. I was doing that for you. We were young and we had a lot of things to figure out. There was one thing I was never unsure of. I loved you. I wanted you to love me too. Instead, you were ashamed and scared. For a long time, I blamed myself. I thought I wasn't good enough. I wasn't pretty enough. I was too weird; too uncool to be the Jayla Barnes. I hated myself for letting you break me, and I hated you for breaking me. Now I realize it wasn't me. It was you. Your own insecurities and fears. Here are my final words to you Jayla. Have a good life because I am no longer in it. No matter how much you come back. We can never be ANYTHING ever again. I no longer hate you, but that you and me; friends are no more. It's better this way. Grow up and get your shit together.

Signed,

Ana.

Analise wrote that letter and burned it. Letting it all go. Letting Jayla go. She was free. Finally, free and also in love.

"Hey love… you been out here for hours." Samaria said coming onto the balcony with her now wife.

"I know I was just thinking." Analise told her.

"About what?" Samaria questioned.

"Us… life." Analise breathed.

"We came along way." Samaria said. Analise nodded overlooking the Arizona mountains.

Yes, Samaria and Analise are now happily married. How'd that happen… That's a story for another lifetime.

ABOUT THE AUTHOR

Ka'Shaun Michelle, also known as Karma, is a twenty-six-year-old, author and radio personality. With a strong passion and strive for telling compelling stories and speaking her mind with strong facts. She's been writing for ten years and in the Broadcasting industry for three years. She has been able to combine both her passions as an upcoming entrepreneur. Ka'Shaun resides in the Midwest where she is currently working on her career with her podcast BlackGirl Magic Radio and her newest release Close Friends. Check out her previously releases available on Amazon: Poisonous: Kiya's Redemption, Poisonous: Looking for Revenge and Diary of Aurora Ciana.